THE OKLAHOMA LAND RUSH

BY MORRIS & GOSCINNY

Original title: Lucky Luke – Ruée sur l'Oklahoma

Translator: Luke Spear
Lettering and text layout: Imadjinn sarl
Printed in Spain by Just Colour Graphic

This edition first published in Great Britain in 2009 by
Cinebook Ltd
56 Beech Avenue
Canterbury, Kent
CT4 7TA
www.cinebook.com

A CIP catalogue record for this book
is available from the British Library

ISBN 978-1-84918-008-5

IN 1830, THE UNITED STATES GOVERNMENT GAVE OKLAHOMA TO THE NATIVE AMERICANS, THUS FREEING UP FOR COLONISATION LANDS THE TRIBES HAD PREVIOUSLY OCCUPIED.
THE CHEROKEE, CREEK, CHICKASAW, CHOCTAW AND SEMINOLE PEOPLES SOON TIRED OF THE DESOLATE GREAT PLAINS OF OKLAHOMA...

UGH...
UGH...
UGH...
UGH...
BY GREAT SACHEM, CHANGE THE SUBJECT!!

THEN, ONE DAY, A LOT LATER, IN THE GOVERNMENTAL OFFICES IN WASHINGTON...
GENTLEMEN, LET'S BUY BACK OKLAHOMA FROM THE INDIANS AND OPEN THAT LAND FOR COLONISATION!

AN EMISSARY WAS DISPATCHED TO OKLAHOMA...

O GREAT CHIEFS, ARE YOU HAPPY IN OKLAHOMA?
NO!

WELL, THEN, BE HAPPY! I'VE BEEN SENT TO BUY BACK THE LAND FROM YOU...

BUY BACK THE LAND FROM US?
BUT WE'RE HAPPY HERE!
IT'S FUN HERE!
YES... WE'LL THINK ABOUT IT...
IT'LL COST YOU!

THE DIRTY DEALING BEGAN WITH GLASS BEADS...

... BUT THE DEED WAS SOON DONE...

IN WASHINGTON...
GENTLEMEN, I HEREBY DECLARE THAT THE OKLAHOMA TERRITORY HAS BEEN BOUGHT BACK FROM THE INDIANS AFTER LABORIOUS NEGOTIATIONS...
OKLAHOMA

... AND SO THE OKLAHOMA TERRITORY IS OPEN FOR COLONISATION!...
BRAVO!
YIPPEE!
HURRAH!

SO THAT ALL THE SETTLERS HAVE AN EQUAL CHANCE AND CAN CHOOSE THE BEST LAND, I SUGGEST THAT ON THE 22ND OF APRIL 1889 (THAT'S MY BIRTHDAY), AT MIDDAY, WE GIVE THE SIGNAL FOR THE OKLAHOMA LAND RUSH...

BUT, SENATOR, FOR EVERYONE TO HAVE AN EQUAL CHANCE, THERE CAN'T BE ANY CHEATERS AND THE TERRITORY MUST REALLY BE EMPTY BEFORE THE DAY OF THE RUSH!...

I'VE ALREADY INVITED THE MAN WHO CAN PREPARE AND WATCH OVER THE WHOLE OPERATION...

ENTER...

MAY I INTRODUCE LUCKY LUKE!

SO, IT IS UNDERSTOOD, LUCKY LUKE: THIS WHOLE HISTORIC OPERATION RESTS ON YOUR SHOULDERS! YOU WILL HAVE THE SUPPORT OF THE GOVERNMENT AND THE CAVALRY...
YOU CAN TRUST ME, SENATOR.

LET'S HEAD OUT FOR OKLAHOMA, JOLLY JUMPER...

AFTER DAYS OF TROUBLE-FREE TRAVELLING...
OKLAHOMA, JOLLY JUMPER... AND WHAT FUN IT IS! AND THE WORST PART IS THAT IF WE MEET ANYONE, WE HAVE TO RUN THEM OUT...

WELL, WELL...

WHAT ARE YOU DOING HERE?
I WAS GOING TO ASK YOU THE SAME...

I DON'T WANT ANY WITNESSES, COWBOY! I HEARD THE SETTLERS WERE COMING, SO I CAME FIRST AND I'VE CHOSEN A GREAT SPOT TO BUILD A SALOON...

YOU WON'T MAKE IT ON YOUR OWN... I'LL GIVE YOU A HAND...

YOU SEE? IT'S A LOT QUICKER WITH TWO OF US...
YEP, THAT'S TRUE...
SALOON

YOU FINISH DOING THE LOCK, AND I'LL FINISH THE DECORATIONS...

HEY! LET ME OUT!...
THE CAVALRY WILL COME TO GET YOU... YOU'VE HAD THE HONOUR OF BUILDING THE FIRST JAIL IN OKLAHOMA...
SALOON
JAIL

LET'S CONTINUE OUR INSPECTION, JOLLY JUMPER...

WELL, WELL...

HAPPY JOYFUL'S
ROLLING STORE
WHISKY
GROCERIES

FINALLY! A CUSTOMER!
HALT!

I CAN OFFER YOU WHISKY, GUITARS, BRACES, WHISKY, SHIRT SNAPS, WHISKY, CAKE SLICES, ...

SAY, FRIEND, WHERE DO YOU THINK YOU ARE?
WELL, IN TEXAS, OF COURSE!...

YOU'RE IN THE OKLAHOMA DESERT, AND YOUR PRESENCE HERE IS ILLEGAL!
THAT'S WHY I HAD NO CUSTOMERS! THIS IS ALL MY HORSE'S FAULT! HE LOVES TO WALK, AND HE CROSSED THE BORDER...

YOU'VE GIVEN ME AN IDEA! I'LL BUY YOUR CARGO, BUT I NEED YOUR HELP!...

HEAD OUT!...

YOUR ROLLING STORE WILL ACT AS BAIT TO CATCH ILLEGAL OCCUPANTS IN THE AREA...
ISN'T... ISN'T THAT DANGEROUS? ...

YES, BUT EFFECTIVE... LOOK, THERE'S A CUSTOMER...

HEY! SHOPKEEPER, I SAW YOUR CART FROM BACK THERE... YOU GOT WHISKY?

NO, BUT I'VE GOT LEAD... GET IN!...

LATER...
UNA BOTELLA DE WEESKI, POR FAVOR...

EVEN LATER...
TWO CASES OF...

LATER STILL...
I...

THIS COULD AFFECT MY REPUTATION WITH MY CLIENTELE...
YES, BUT YOU DO HAVE THE HONOUR OF DRIVING OKLAHOMA'S FIRST PRISON WAGON... WELL, HERE'S THE BORDER.

OKLAHOMA TERRITORY ENTRY FORBIDDEN
I WANT A LAWYER!
CAN I AT LEAST GET A WHISKY?
ESO! WEESKI!
I'VE BROUGHT YOU CARGO, CAPTAIN! THE TERRITORY SHOULD BE MORE OR LESS EMPTY NOW... THERE'S ONE IN JAIL STILL TO BE PICKED UP...
HAPPY JOYFUL'S MOBILE STORE WHISKY GROCERIES

THE FIRST CANDIDATES FOR THE RUSH HAVE ALREADY ARRIVED... LET'S TAKE A PEEK AT THE CAMP...

THAT GUY GOT HERE FIRST; THEY CALL HIM SPEEDY JONES... HE RARELY GETS OFF HIS HORSE, EVEN THOUGH HE STILL HAS WEEKS TO WAIT... SPEEDY KNOWS THAT HE'LL BE FIRST; HE SWORE HE'D BE THE FIRST!...
OKLAHOMA
ENTRY
FORBIDDEN

OKLAHOMA
ENTRY
FORBIDDEN

THAT GUY THERE, ON HIS OWN, ALSO WANTS TO BE ONE OF THE FIRST... LET'S NOT DISTURB HIM... HE'S TAKING A SIESTA...

IT'S GOING TO BE DIFFICULT TO BRING ANY ORDER TO ALL THIS...

THE MOST DIFFICULT THING WILL BE TO STOP THE SOONERS...
THE SOONERS?

YES, THE SOONERS ARE THE SNEAKY ONES WHO TRY TO CROSS THE BORDER BEFORE THE OPENING DAY SO THEY CAN AUCTION OFF THE BEST LAND AT THEIR LEISURE...

AND, INDEED, IN HIS TENT, THE ONE THEY CALLED BEASTLY BLUBBER...

HEH HEH!... THERE'S NO MOON TONIGHT... WITH THIS MAKEUP AND THESE BLACK CLOTHES, I'LL BE INVISIBLE... I'LL CROSS THE BORDER...

THAT NIGHT...

OUCH!
HEY!

EXCUSE ME... I DIDN'T SEE YOU THERE...

WELL, WELL... THAT COULD BE A SOONER...

I'LL PRACTICE SHOOTING IN THE DARK...
!

HEY! DON'T BE STUPID!!

I THOUGHT I HEARD A VOICE... BAH! I'LL KEEP SHOOTING...
WAIT, DARNIT! I'M GETTING SOME LIGHT CLOTHES OUT OF MY BAG!

JAIL
!

YOU SEE, DOPEY? BEASTLY BLUBBER WAS CAUGHT 'CUZ HE HAD NO PLAN AND NO BOSS!...
YES, COYOTE WILL...

BUT WE'LL CROSS THAT BORDER AND YOU KNOW WHY?
BECAUSE YOU'RE THE BOSS, COYOTE WILL...

HERE'S MY PLAN, DOPEY: YOU'LL ATTACH COOKING PANS TO YOUR SADDLE. WHEN YOU GET YOUR HORSE TO GALLOP, THE PANS WILL MAKE SUCH AN INFERNAL RACKET THAT LUCKY LUKE AND HIS SOLDIERS WILL FOLLOW YOU...

MEANWHILE, I'LL JUST STROLL OVER THE BORDER IN ANOTHER SPOT!
THAT'S A GREAT PLAN! THAT'S A REALLY GREAT PLAN!

BUT... ERM... ME? I'LL BE CAPTURED!

THAT'S PART OF THE PLAN, DOPEY!!

WHILE YOU GO QUIETLY TO JAIL, I'LL SECURE SOME GOOD LAND! I'LL MAKE IT PRODUCTIVE, AND WHEN YOU'RE FREE, YOU'LL BE RICH BECAUSE I'LL SHARE IT WITH YOU!...
THAT'S A GREAT PLAN! THAT'S A REALLY GREAT PLAN!

YOU'RE SO GENEROUS, COYOTE WILL!! THANK YOU!
THAT BOY'S STUPIDITY WILL NEVER CEASE TO AMAZE ME!

MORRIS

EVERYTHING'S READY, COYOTE WILL, EVERYTHING'S READY!
SHHHH!

COME ON, SADDLE UP! YOU HEAD WEST AND I'LL HEAD EAST!

?
CLANG
CLONG
BLAMM
BLING

DOPEY SHOULD ALREADY HAVE LUCKY LUKE AND THE WHOLE CAVALRY ON HIS HEELS WITH ALL THAT DIN!...
CLANG
CLING!
BLING

THAT IMBECILE DOPEY GOT THE WRONG HORSE!!!

WELL, THEN, FRIEND, WHAT'S ALL THIS NOISE ABOUT?... MAY I REMIND YOU THAT YOU'RE ON THE WRONG SIDE OF THE BORDER?...

I HAVE TO SAY THAT I DON'T UNDERSTAND THE TRICK...
JAIL

COYOTE WILL BETRAYED ME! HE TOOK THE PANS INSTEAD OF ME! HE WANTS TO GO TO JAIL AND JUST WAIT AROUND WHILE I TAKE ALL THE RISKS!

COYOTE WILL BETRAYED ME. BUT HE WON'T GET AWAY WITH IT!

?
JAIL
HEY! ARREST ME! I'M A SOONER! I TRIED TO CROSS THE BORDER!

I HAVE TO ADMIT THAT I STILL DON'T UNDERSTAND...

JUST PERFECT! YOU WANTED TO GO TO JAIL INSTEAD OF ME SO THAT I WAS THE ONE TAKING ALL THE RISKS! WELL, NO! WE'LL GET RICH TOGETHER IN JAIL!...

IT'S NOT THAT GREAT IN HERE! WE HAVE TO ESCAPE...

I'VE GOT A PLAN, BEASTLY BLUBBER! YOU'RE A BIG GUY... YOU CAN BREAK THROUGH ONE OF THE PRISON WALLS...
THAT'S A GREAT PLAN! THAT'S A REALLY GREAT PLAN!!

... AS SOON AS YOU OPEN A WAY THROUGH, ROPEY WILL ESCAPE! THE GUARDS WILL CHASE HIM AND WE'LL MAKE A RUN FOR IT...

CRACK

CRACK!

CHASE ME! I AM ESCAPING! YOOHOO! I'M ESCAPING!!

CHASE ME!!
YOOHOO!!
I'VE ESCAPED!
THOSE JAILBIRDS ARE STARTING TO ANNOY ME...
?

GO ON, THEN!...
I'M STUCK!

WHAT ARE YOU DOING?!... PUSH!
SHUT UP! YOU HAVE NO IDEA...

THIS JAIL ISN'T ONE OF THE MOST SOLID... BUT THAT OUGHT TO HOLD YOU...
GOOD IDEA TO GET SO FAT!
IT'S NOT MY FAULT! EVERYTHING I EAT GOES STRAIGHT TO MY WAIST!

WHAT ABOUT DOPEY? WILL YOU LET HIM GET AWAY?...
HIM? HE'LL COME BACK TO JAIL ON HIS OWN... HE LIKES IT HERE...

FOLLOW ME! YOOHOO! I'VE ESCAPED!

YOOH....!...

COYOTE WILL DUPED ME AGAIN!! HE'S LOUNGING AROUND IN JAIL AND EXPECTS ME TO WORK TO MAKE HIM RICH...
WE'RE NOT PLAYING ANY-MORE?...

I WANT TO GO BACK TO JAIL!...
I'VE BEEN WAITING FOR YOU...

OH, YEAH! YOU TRIED TO BETRAY ME!...
LET GO OF MY NECK, IMBECILE!

COME QUICK, LUKE! THERE'S A FIGHT IN THE SALOON!

LET ME THROUGH!
SALOON

WHO ARE YOU?... WHAT'S GOING ON?...
I'M SMITH... JOHN SMITH...

I WAS PLAYING POKER WITH THAT GUY THEY CALL FLASH BINGO... HE WON MY MONEY, MY HORSES AND MY CART... I ACCUSED HIM OF CHEATING... SO HE GOT ANGRY!...

THE MONEY ISN'T A PROBLEM... BUT WITHOUT THE HORSES AND CART, I CAN'T JOIN IN THE RUSH...

FLASH BINGO?... LOOKS LIKE YOU'RE CHEATING...
YEAH! I HATE GAMES OF CHANCE...
AND I HATE CHEATERS! I DON'T WANT ANY IN OKLAHOMA!...

GENTLEMEN, PLEASE, DON'T FIGHT! ALL I'VE GOT LEFT INTACT IS THIS BARREL OF BEER...

DON'T DRAW, LUKE! I'M NOT ARMED...

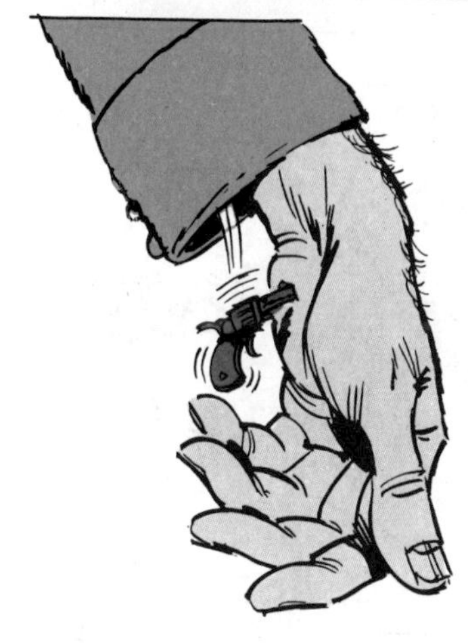

BANG! ...

THE HAMMER!... HE BROKE THE HAMMER!...

MORRIS
YOU DON'T ARGUE WITH GUYS LIKE THAT!...

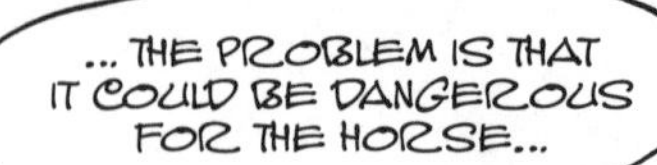

JONES SABOTAGED MARTIN'S CART... WHILE MARTIN SABOTAGED JONES'S CART...

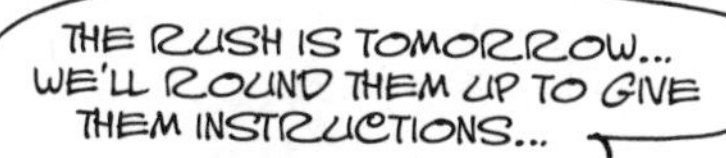

*THAT'S WHY THE SETTLERS CAME TO BE CALLED "BOOMERS."

COCK-A-DOODLE-DOO...

AAAH!... IT'S THE DAWN OF THE BIG DAY, JOLLY JUMPER...

LET'S GO SEE IF EVERYTHING'S READY FOR THE RUSH...

HEY, LUKE! WHAT ABOUT US?...
WE'LL LET YOU OUT AFTER THE RUSH... IF THERE'S ANY LAND LEFT, YOU CAN HAVE IT...
16A

WE'LL MEET AGAIN, LUCKY LUKE!...

EVERYTHING'S READY, LUKE!...
THE WOMEN AND CHILDREN ARE AT THE BACK. THE MEN ARE ON THE STARTING LINE.

16B

IT'S ALMOST TIME, LUKE!...
I'LL HEAD OVER TO THEM...

WHEN THE SHADOW DISAPPEARS, IT WILL BE DEAD ON NOON, THE TIME FOR THE SIGNAL...

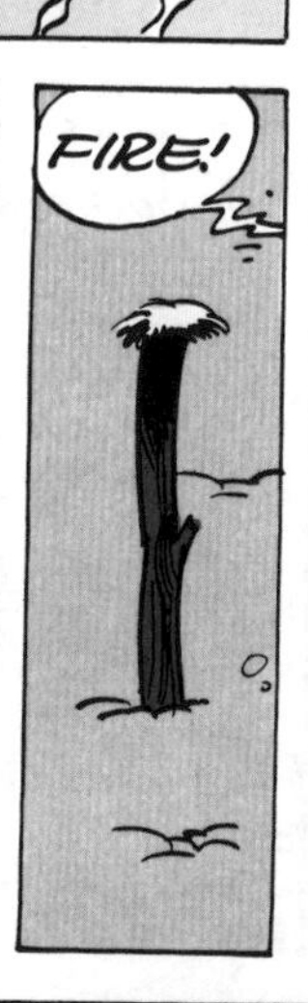
FIRE!

BOOMMMM

AND THEY'RE OFF!!

IN A ROLL OF THUNDEROUS NOISE, THE RUSH FOR OKLAHOMA BEGAN! ALL THE BOOMERS WERE AWAY...

... WELL... NEARLY ALL...
ZZZZZ
ZZZZ
OKLAHOMA
ZZZZZ
ZZZZZZ

AFTER THEM, JOLLY JUMPER!...

MARTIN
EEEEK!...
HAHAHA!...
JONES

HAHAHA!...
MARTIN
EEEEK!...
JONES
CRACK

OLD TIMER'S PROPERTY

I'M PULLING OUT THE BIG GUNS!...
LET ME THROUGH OR I'LL SHOOT!...
18A

NONE OF THAT, BUDDY!...

NO NEED TO GO ANY FURTHER...
THIS LAND WILL SUIT ME...
SCREEEEEE

ARE YOU HAPPY, GRANDDAD?...
OLD TIMER'S PROPERTY

GET OFF MY PROPERTY, BOY!!!!...
BANG
BANG
18B

THE BOOMERS CHOSE THEIR LAND, WHICH DIDN'T ALWAYS GO SMOOTHLY...
MARTIN'S PROPERTY

WHOSE?
JONES'S PROPERTY

I WAS HERE FIRST!!

SMITH'S PROPERTY

LET'S SEE IF EVERYTHING'S GOING WELL...

KID BULLET'S PROPERTY
Walking on grass prohibited under pain of death!

REVOLTING WILLIAMS'S PROPERTY
Look out! This is mine. Eli's!

DIGGER THOMPSON'S PROPERTY
Stranger, walk on this land and you'll find yourself six feet under

PISTOL PETE'S PROPERTY
I'm gonna plant wheat in this ground and lead in anyone who walks over it!...

JOLLY, OLD BOY, I THINK WE'VE GOT OUR WORK CUT OUT FOR US...
MORRIS

GET OUT OF HERE!
IT'S MY LAND, USURPER!

COME ON, FRIENDS! CALM DOWN!
GET OFF MY LAND!
DON'T STAY ON MINE!

WHAT'S THIS?
THEY'RE LINING UP FOR THE LAWYER TO RESOLVE THEIR DISPUTES...
OKLAHOMA IS A PARADISE...

WE'LL NEED TO FIND SOMEWHERE TO SLEEP, JOLLY JUMPER... ALL THE LAND'S TAKEN...

HEY! WILL YOU LET ME STAY ON YOUR LAND WITH MY HORSE FOR THE NIGHT?
HMMM...
OWNER: FOXY SPARROW

OK... $5!...
THAT'S EXPENSIVE, BUT I DON'T HAVE A CHOICE...

MORRIS
OWNER: FOXY SPARROW
OKLAHOMA
PALACE HOTEL
5 BUCKS A NIGHT

WAIT FOR ME THERE, JOLLY JUMPER. THIS MORNING I'M GOING TO TAKE A WALK...

ON THIS FORMERLY DESERTED PLAIN, THE BOOMVILLE "BOOMTOWN" WAS TAKING SHAPE...
DRUGS

SPECULATORS ARGUED OVER LAND FOR FORTUNES...
$1,000 FOR YOUR LAND, ROCKWELL...
DEAL!...

... PRICES ROSE AT A DIZZYING PACE...
I'LL TAKE BACK THE LAND FOR $5,000...
DEAL!

GOOD MOVE...
EXCELLENT DEAL...

RESTAURANTS MADE A FORTUNE...
JOE! MINCE ME UP ANOTHER COW!
FRESH HAMBURGERS

IT'S GOING CRAZY! I'LL GO GET JOLLY JUMPER AND TAKE A RIDE AROUND THE COUNTRY...

OKLAHOMA
PALACE HOTEL
FOKY SPARROW, OWNER
!

AND WHAT WERE YOU THINKING, LEAVING YOUR HORSE IN A HOTEL? YOU OWE ME A DOOR!
MORRIS

YOU'LL SEE, JOLLY JUMPER... BUILDING IS GOING AT A CRAZY PACE...

WHAT ARE YOU DOING HERE?...
WE'RE WAITING FOR THE TEACHER TO FINISH BUILDING THE SCHOOL...

HEY, BOYS! THEY'RE BUILDING A SALOON!...

DON'T GET ANGRY, GENTLEMEN. WE'RE PUTTING THE BAR IN NEXT...
22A

CONSTRUCTION WAS QUICK, BUT NOT ALWAYS VERY SOLID...
FINISHED!... NOW ALL I HAVE LEFT TO DO IS TO PUT UP GRANDPA'S PORTRAIT...

THE TOWN WAS NEARLY FINISHED, BUT THEY FORGOT ONE DETAIL...
NO STREETS!... WE'LL HAVE TO DEMOLISH THE HOUSES AND LAY OUT SOME STREETS...
BUT LUKE, IS THAT REALLY NECESSARY?... IT'S IN THE STREETS THAT ALL THE ACCIDENTS HAPPEN...
HOTEL
MORRIS
22B

EXCUSE ME, SIR, IS THIS A BANK YOU'RE BUILDING?...
YES...

OH, GOOD!...

IS IT NEARLY DONE?
YES, YES, MY FRIEND...

THERE... COME IN, SIR
THANK YOU, SIR...

NOW! OPEN THE SAFE!

A NEW BANK CALLS FOR NEW BANDITS...

THAT'S WHAT I THOUGHT...

NEW BANDITS CALL FOR A NEW JAIL... YOU'LL BUILD IT JUST HOW YOU LIKE IT.

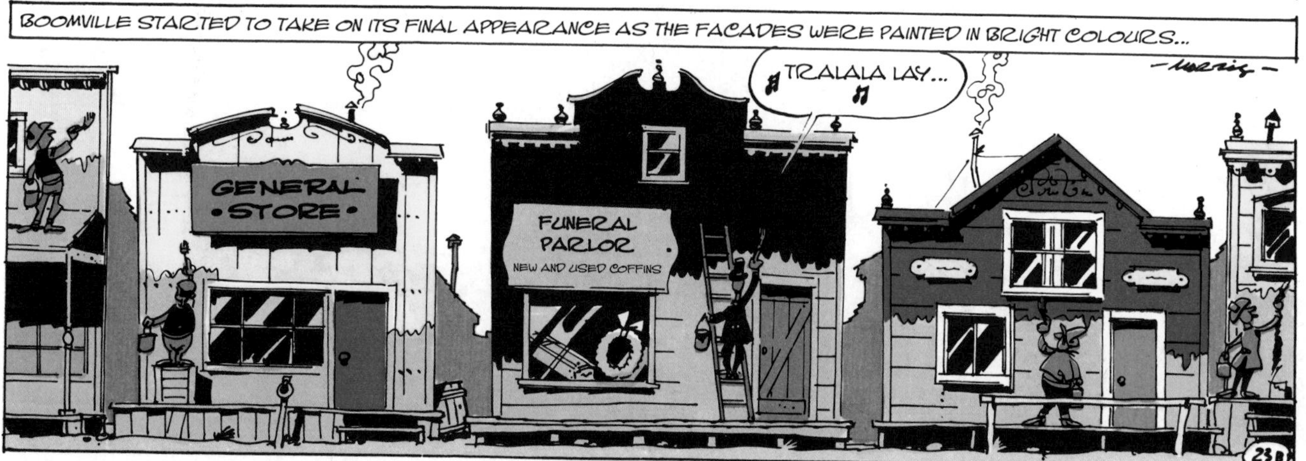
BOOMVILLE STARTED TO TAKE ON ITS FINAL APPEARANCE AS THE FACADES WERE PAINTED IN BRIGHT COLOURS...
TRALALA LAY...
GENERAL STORE
FUNERAL PARLOR
NEW AND USED COFFINS

THE SETTLERS WERE NOT PEACEFUL PEOPLE, AND REVOLVERS WERE DRAWN QUICKLY IN BOOMVILLE...

THIS CAN'T GO ON...

CARRYING GUNS FORBIDDEN IN BOOMVILLE
ALL CITIZENS MUST BRING THEIR GUNS TO LUCKY LUKE BEFORE NOON TODAY.
FOR THE TEMPORARY GOVERNMENT OF BOOMVILLE
Lucky Luke

THIS LAW IS SCANDALOUS! IT'S SCANDALOUS! SCANDALOUS, I TELL YA!...
CALM DOWN, BUSTER! LUCKY LUKE'S RIGHT...
24 A

A REAL SCANDAL!!
I COULDN'T AGREE MORE, BUSTER!
FUNERAL PARLOUR
BUSTER'S GUNS

... NINE, AND 10... THAT'S THE LOT...

OH, I FEEL SO LIGHT, SO LIGHT...
I HOPE THAT WE'LL GET SOME PEACE NOW...

BUT LUCKY LUKE WAS WRONG...
HOTEL
24 B

SAY, BEASTLY BLUBBER, DID YOU NOTICE THEY AIN'T CARRYING ANY GUNS?
YEAH, IT AIN'T RIGHT!...

HEY! FRIEND, WHY ARE PEOPLE WALKING AROUND WITHOUT GUNS?...

IT'S ONE OF LUCKY LUKE'S LAWS... HE OUTLAWED ALCOHOL AND GAMBLING, TOO...
LUCKY LUKE? HIM AGAIN!!...

TO THE SALOON! I HAVE AN IDEA...
25A

WHISKY!
NO WHISKY!...

SAY, IS IT TRUE THAT ALL GUNS HAVE BEEN CONFISCATED?
YEAH...

SO, YOU DON'T HAVE ANY GUNS?
NO...

PERFECT! THEN I WANT TO BUY YOUR SALOON! I'LL SET THE PRICE!

THE SALOON OWNER'S LEAVING BOOMVILLE... STRANGE...
25B

WELL, IF IT ISN'T COYOTE WILL, BEASTLY BLUBBER AND DOPEY! SO, THEY LET YOU OUT OF JAIL?...
OUR FIRST CUSTOMER! WHAT A PLEASURE!...

ENOUGH JOKING AROUND! YOU KNOW THE LAW: NO ALCOHOL, NO GAMBLING!...

OK. I'M LEAVING, BUT I'VE GOT MY EYE ON YOU...
AH, LUKE, YOU'RE SUCH A BORE...

HOHO HEE HO...
HEE HEE
WHAT'S SO FUNNY? WHAT'S SO FUNNY?

OKAY! TO WORK! THIS TOWN'S GOING TO MAKE US RICH! WE'LL ORGANISE AN UNDERGROUND GAMBLING DEN!...
AND I'LL MAKE THE ALCOHOL!

IT'S A RECIPE THAT I GOT FROM MY MOTHER! YOU CAN TELL ME WHAT YOU THINK!
PRIVATE

PRIVATE
WHAMM..

YEAH, MY FRIEND DECIDED TO MAKE US SOME FLAMBÉED PANCAKES...

I MUST HAVE OVERDONE THE MIX...
LUCKILY THE DAMAGES WEREN'T TOO SERIOUS...

I'LL GET BACK TO WORK...
YEAH, BUT BE CAREFUL...

SOON AFTER...
THIS TIME I GOT IT!

YEAH, BUT WHO'LL TASTE IT?...

... LA LALALA LAA...
27A

TASTE THIS, DOPEY! IT'LL BRING YOU AROUND!!

GLUG GLUG GLUG...

HIC!

YIPPEE! IT WORKED!!
SHH! A CUSTOMER!...

SIR?...
A LEMONADE...
MORRIS

AFTER A COUPLE OF GLASSES OF "LEMONADE"...
HEY! BOYS!... HIC! COME AND TASTE COYOTE WILL'S LEMONADE!
27B

YIPPEE!... SWEET GENEVIEVE, BEAUTIFUL GENEVIEEEEEVE... LONG LIVE... LEMONADE!

WHAT ARE YOU DRINKING?...
MELONADE... LAMONEDE... LOMA... HIC!...

HEY, COYOTE WILL! LUCKY LUKE'S HERE...
YOU KNOW MY INSTRUCTIONS. GIVE THEM TO DOPEY!
28▲

DOPEY! SERVE ALCOHOL TO EVERYONE AND LEMONADE TO LUCKY LUKE...
YES... YES, YES...

DOPEY! A LEMONADE!
LET'S SEE... LEMONADE FOR EVERYONE, ALCOHOL FOR LUCKY LUKE... NO!... ALCOHOL FOR LUCKY LUKE, LEMONADE FOR...
TWO LEMONADES, PLEASE! HURRY!

GULP
GULP
GULP
GULP

THIS IS LEMONADE!...
COYOTE WILL! PUT YOUR CARD GAME ON HOLD! I'VE SERVED LUKE THE ALCOHOL BEASTLY MADE...
28B

SALOON
TH...THE... HIC...THERE'S... HIC... GONNA BE A RUCKUS...
TA... TA... TAKE COVER!

WHAT'S GOING ON?
I... I MADE A LITTLE MISTAKE...

WE DON'T LIKE TROUBLEMAKERS, LUCKY LUKE!

ALL THE MORE PROOF THAT WE'RE NOT GUILTY! COYOTE WILL TOLD ME TO SERVE YOU LEMONADE! IT WAS JUST A MISTAKE...

YOUR NUMBER'S UP! THE SALE OF ALCOHOL AND AN UNDER-GROUND GAMING ROOM!

DON'T WASTE YOUR LEAD, COYOTE WILL! I'LL HANDLE THIS!

WHACK

DON'T TOUCH YOUR GUNS, COYOTE WILL!...
BANG
BANG

SALO
LET'S DESTROY THIS DEN OF INIQUITY, LADIES!

LUCKY LUKE, DON'T YOU THINK THE TIME HAS COME TO CHOOSE A MAYOR FOR THE CITY?
GENTLEMEN, YOU'RE RIGHT. I'LL CALL A MEETING!

CITIZENS OF BOOMVILLE
MEETING
TONIGHT AT THE SALOON TO ARRANGE
ELECTIONS
FOR A
PERMANENT GOVERNMENT
FOR THE TEMPORARY GOVERNMENT OF BOOMVILLE
Lucky Luke

GENTLEMEN, WE'RE GOING TO ORGANISE ELECTIONS TO CHOOSE A MAYOR... MY ROLE IN BOOMVILLE WILL BE FINISHED AS SOON AS YOU HAVE A SOLID GOVERNMENT THAT CAN UPHOLD THE LAW!...
AS AN UNDERTAKER, I CAN'T STAND ESTABLISHED ORDER...
I SHARE YOUR OPINION, AS A GUN STORE OWNER...

THE CANDIDATES STARTED THEIR ELECTORAL CAMPAIGN...
VOTE FOR OLD TIMER! AND FOR A YOUNG GOVERNMENT!

VOTE FOR FATS WILLIAMS
ENOUGH TO EAT FOR EVERYONE!

FOR THE GREAT
STATURE OF OUR CITY,
VOTE TOM THUMB!

I WONDER IF THERE AREN'T TOO MANY CANDIDATES... THIS COULD CAUSE CONFLICTS...

VOTE FOR PEACE WITH JONES!
VOTE FOR A PEACEFUL LIFE! WITH MARTIN!

TRAITOR!
SELL-OUT!

LIAR!
CITIZENS, IF YOU VOTE FOR ME, I CAN ASSURE YOU THAT EVERYONE WILL HAVE WHAT THEY NEED TO MAKE SOUP!
SWINDLER!
CROOK!

I DON'T KNOW IF THEY'LL HAVE ANY SOUP, BUT I'VE GOT WHAT I NEED...

AN ENERGETIC GOVERNMENT WITH SMITTY!

SMITTY!

I ALREADY TOLD YOU THAT I NEED WOOD FOR THE FIRE!

BUT, DARLING, THE GREATNESS OF OUR LAND... MY SACRED OBLIGATIONS AS A CITIZEN... MY MISSION...

THAT'S ONE WAY TO NIP A GLORIOUS CAREER IN THE BUD!
AN ENERGETIC GOVERNMENT WITH
SMITTY!

HEY! LUCKY LUKE!

YOU HAVE TO SET US FREE! WE HAVE A RIGHT TO VOTE, TOO!

YOU'VE GOT A GOOD POINT...

OK, OUT! THAT WAY YOU CAN VOTE FOR THE GOVERNMENT THAT'LL PUT YOU BACK IN PRISON...

WELL... ARE YOU COMING, DOPEY?

I'LL LEAVE, BUT I DON'T WANT TO!... PRISON IS THE ONLY PLACE WHERE I DON'T HAVE ANY PROBLEMS!...

VOTE
WELL, LOOKY HERE! THE PLACE IS BUZZING!
YEP! THREE QUARTERS OF THE POPULATION HAVE NOMINATED THEMSELVES TO BE MAYOR...
VOT
SM

CAN ANYONE NOMINATE HIMSELF?...
SEEMS LIKE IT...

HEY, DOPEY! WHERE YOU GOING?...
I'LL BE RIGHT BACK...

Vote for Dopey

HAHA!... HEEHEE!! HE'S FUNNY!
HOHOHOHO!... HOW ARE YOU, YOUR HONOUR?
Vote for Dopey

DOPEY'S CANDIDACY AMUSED EVERYONE...
GO, DOPEY!
DOPEY FOR MAYOR!

BUT SOMETHING STRANGE HAPPENED...
RATHER THAN VOTE FOR YOU, I'LL VOTE FOR THAT CRETIN, DOPEY!!
... SURPRISING, EVEN.
DOPEY'S AS SMART AS YOU ARE!
AND YOU'RE AS DUMB AS DOPEY!
DOPEY'S NAME WAS ON EVERY-ONE'S LIPS...
YOU INFER-NAL DOPEY!
DOPEY YOUR-SELF!
DON'T BE A DOPEY!...

BE QUICK SETTING UP THE TENT! IT'S THE POLLING STATION, AND THE ELECTIONS ARE TOMORROW...

EVERYTHING'S READY... LET'S GO TO BED! TOMORROW BOOMVILLE WILL HAVE A MAYOR!...

BOOMVILLE SLEPT... BUT A LOT OF CITIZENS DREAMT OF GLORY AND POWER...

ELECTION DAY CAME...
VOTE GONZALEZ
VOTE CULLIFORD
VOTE JONES
POLLING STATION
VOTE
VOTE SMITH

WHISKY

NEXT!...

VOTED

IT'S NO GOOD!... I'VE ALREADY TRIED... THE INK IS INDELIBLE! YOU CAN ONLY VOTE ONCE.

THE CANDIDATES WERE SO SURE OF THEIR SUCCESS THAT THEY HAD ALREADY PREPARED THEIR SPEECHES...
"MY DEAREST CITIZENS..."
BRAVO, YOUR HONOUR!

THE LAST VOTER HAS VOTED AND THE ELECTIONS ARE OVER... I'LL NOW COUNT THE VOTES!

IT TAKES SO LONG...
I BET $10 ON ME!
$20 ON ME!

SHHH! HERE'S LUCKY LUKE! HE'S GOING TO ANNOUNCE THE RESULTS!...

GENTLEMEN, BY A VERY LARGE MAJORITY, MR. DOPEY HAS BEEN VOTED MAYOR OF BOOMVILLE!!...

WHAT?...
THAT'S NOT POSSIBLE!
I VOTED FOR HIM, BUT IT WAS JUST A JOKE!...
ME, TOO!
CANCEL THE ELECTION!
WHAT A DISGRACE!

SILENCE! THE ELECTIONS WERE FREE AND HONEST! DOPEY IS THE MAYOR OF BOOMVILLE. YOU HAVE ELECTED HIM!
35A

MATTER OF FACT, WHERE IS DOPEY?...

HE PASSED OUT!...
?

COME ON, MR MAYOR, YOU CAN TAKE YOUR OFFICE IN THE TOWN HALL!

WHERE AM I? I HAD A STRANGE DREAM... I DREAMT THAT DOPEY WAS ELECTED... WHERE IS DOPEY?...
IN THE TOWN HALL...

HEY!
COYOTE WILL! COME ON, COYOTE, BUDDY!...
35B

TOWN HALL
I'LL HELP YOU GET STARTED...

YOUR OFFICE, SEÑOR MAYOR...

AND NOW, WHAT ARE YOUR ORDERS, MR. MAYOR?...

I WOULD LIKE TO BE PUT BACK IN PRISON...
THAT'S IMPOSSIBLE FOR NOW, BUT I'M SURE IT'LL HAPPEN LATER...

DOPEY, YOU HAVE TO FORGET YOUR OLD LIFE AND SHOW YOURSELF WORTHY OF THE HONOUR BESTOWED UPON YOU YOU'RE THE FIRST MAYOR OF BOOMVILLE!

YOU'RE RIGHT, LUCKY LUKE! I'LL BE A GOOD AND TRUE MAYOR!... FOR AS LONG AS I HOLD THIS OFFICE, SAFETY WILL REIGN IN THE STREETS OF BOOMVILLE!!
THAT'S RIGHT!!

VUESTRO HONOR, THE SEÑORES COYOTE WILL AND BEASTLY BLUBBER ARE ASKING TO SEE YOU

THE MAYOR CANNOT GIVE YOU AN AUDIENCE NOW... PLEASE WAIT...
AUDIENCE?... WAIT?!...

YOU'LL SEE!...
CALM DOWN, COYOTE! LET'S BE DIPLOMATIC!

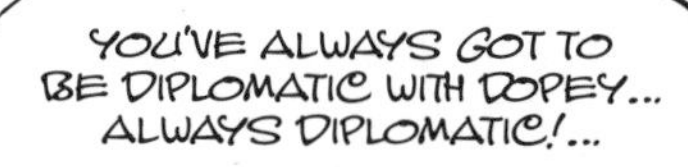
YOU'VE ALWAYS GOT TO BE DIPLOMATIC WITH DOPEY... ALWAYS DIPLOMATIC!...

THE MAYOR WILL SEE YOU NOW...
YOU'LL SEE... LET ME HANDLE THIS...

HEY, GOOD OLD DOPEY!...

I'M NOT "GOOD OLD DOPEY," I'M YOUR HONOUR THE MAYOR...

YOU'LL SEE WHAT I DO WITH YOUR HONOUR!...
DIPLOMATIC, BEASTLY... ALWAYS DIPLOMATIC...

ENOUGH GAMES, BOYS. LISTEN HERE! I'VE GOT PLANS FOR US ALL! WE'LL GET RICH ON BOOMVILLE'S MONEY!...

... HEY! AN IDEA: LET'S RAISE A TAX TO BUILD A ROAD.

OF COURSE, WE'LL SHARE THE TAX MONEY AND WE WON'T BUILD A ROAD!!
THAT'S TERRIBLE!

A ROAD? THAT ISN'T A BAD IDEA AT ALL...

SOON...
HERE'S A ROAD THAT WON'T COST THE CITIZENS A DIME...

TIME WENT BY. TO EVERYONE'S SURPRISE, DOPEY WAS A GOOD—EVEN AN EXCELLENT—MAYOR. THE TOWN HARVESTED THE FRUITS OF AN HONEST ADMINISTRATION, AND DOPEY WON THE RESPECT OF HIS FELLOW CITIZENS.
STORE
BANK

BUT NOT EVERYONE WAS SATISFIED IN BOOMVILLE... A BARN HOUSED THE UNHAPPY...

IT'S GOING BADLY...
YEAH. SO MUCH PROSPERITY...

WE HAVE TO TRY A TAKEOVER! A REVOLUTION! TAKE THE POWER FROM LUCKY LUKE AND DOPEY'S HANDS! WE HAVE TO BRING THE MALCONTENTS TOGETHER AND APPEAL TO THE WEAK-HEARTED TO JOIN US!...

IT WON'T BE EASY TO UNITE THE UNHAPPY! THINGS ARE GOING PRETTY WELL...

FRIENDS, FRIENDS, YOU'RE DESPAIRING TOO SOON! I HAPPEN TO HAVE SOME GOOD NEWS!
NOT EVERYTHING'S LOOKING GOOD ON THE HORIZON...

THE OKLAHOMA LAND RUSH ATTRACTED TOO MANY PEOPLE. NEW SETTLERS ARE ARRIVING EVERY DAY ON THIS DRY LAND WHERE SEEDS DON'T GROW...

FOOD'S GETTING RARER! THERE'S NOT ENOUGH WATER, AND IN THE WELLS THEY DIG, THEY'RE JUST FINDING A THICK, BLACK LIQUID... SOME CALL IT OIL. IN ANY CASE, IT'S NOT DRINKABLE...

OH, YES, MY FRIENDS! OH, YES! THERE WILL BE UNHAPPY FOLK!...
LET'S PUBLISH A NEWSPAPER TO EXPOSE THE FACTS...
WELL DONE, UNDERTAKER!

THE DROUGHT WAS SOON FELT...
MOOOO!... MOOOO!...

MOOOO!... MOOOO!...

THE DROP EVAPORATED BEFORE IT EVEN TOUCHED THE BOTTOM...
MOOOO!... MOOOO!...

IT GIVES A FUNNY TASTE TO THE MILK, BUT AT LEAST IT'S FOAMY...
MOOOOHIC!...
BEER

THE CROWS FLEW OVER EMPTY FIELDS... ALL THEY FOUND WAS THE SCARECROW'S STRAW...

FOOD BECAME UNAFFORDABLE...
A HAM SANDWICH, PLEASE...
THAT'S $50...

UGH! THE BREAD'S STALE AND COVERED IN DUST!...
OF COURSE! IT'S IMPORTED FROM TEXAS...

FAMINE WAS RIFE...
I'VE MANAGED TO FIND A PIECE OF LARD... IF ONLY I COULD FIND SOME BEANS...

I'VE GOT SOME BEANS... WITH A PIECE OF LARD, THAT WOULD MAKE A MEAL...

WANT TO TRADE?
THAT WOULDN'T SOLVE OUR PROBLEM... LET'S SHARE INSTEAD...

THE PROBLEM IS THAT ONE RATION OF LARD AND ONE RATION OF BEANS DOESN'T MAKE TWO RATIONS OF BAKED BEANS...

I HAVE TO WARN DOPEY THAT THINGS AREN'T GOING WELL...
TOWN HALL

THE SITUATION'S GETTING SERIOUS, DOPEY...
BUT THE PEOPLE LOVE ME...

OH!...
LET ME SEE...

CITIZENS!
RISE UP AGAINST THE INIQUITOUS GOVERNMENT!
• WE HAVE NO WATER OR SUPPLIES!
• THE LAND WON'T GROW ANYTHING!
• WHOSE FAULT IS IT?
• THE INIQUITY OF MAYOR DOPEY AND THE INIQUITOUS LUCKY LUKE!
CITIZENS, UNITE AGAINST THEIR INIQUITY!
VALUES!

THIS... THIS IS INIQUITY!...
AND OUT THERE, EVERYBODY'S READING THIS PAPER...
40A

I THINK THERE'S GOING TO BE TROUBLE...
REVOLUTION?...

IN THE CONSPIRATORS' DEN, FURIOUS WORK WAS CARRIED OUT ON A CAMPAIGN OF RABBLE-ROUSING...
HEY! UNDERTAKER, PRINT THIS UP IN LARGE CHARACTERS AND WITH NO MISTAKES!

AREN'T YOU OVERDOING THE "INIQUITY" WORD A LITTLE? SINCE YOU FOUND IT IN THE DICTIONARY, YOU'VE BEEN USING IT ALL THE TIME...

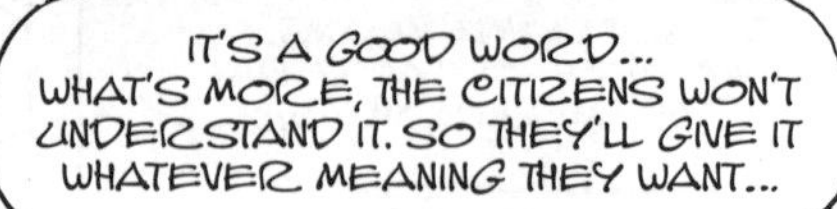
IT'S A GOOD WORD... WHAT'S MORE, THE CITIZENS WON'T UNDERSTAND IT. SO THEY'LL GIVE IT WHATEVER MEANING THEY WANT...

MORRIS
40B

THINGS ARE TAKING A TURN FOR THE WORSE! A PROTEST!...

DOPEY AND LUCKY LUKE ARE INIQUITOUS
LET'S HUNT THE INIQUI-TOUS!
IT'S ALWAYS THE SAME ONES THAT INIQUIT!
DOPEY! LUKE! ENOUGH INIQUITY!
TOWN HALL
41A

PREPARE TO DEFEND YOURSELF, DOPEY!...

BUT AT THAT VERY MOMENT, SOMETHING UNEXPECTED OCCURRED... A VIOLENT WIND CARRYING CLOUDS OF RED, BURNING SAND...

THAT SANDSTORM WILL RUIN THE FEW PLANTS IN OKLAHOMA AND MAKE THE WELLS UNUSABLE...

DOPEY, I THINK WE'RE SAVED, BUT THIS TOWN IS DEAD...
I'VE SEEN TOWNS LOSE THEIR MAYOR BEFORE, BUT A MAYOR LOSING HIS TOWN...

IT'S WORKING! LET'S GO AND STIR UP THE RIOT!...
WHAT A WIND!
LOOK!

HEY, COMRADE, WHERE ARE YOU GOING? AREN'T YOU COMING TO REVOLT?
NO! I'M LEAVING OKLAHOMA! TOO MUCH MISERY... I PREFER TO GO SOMEWHERE ELSE, WHATEVER THE GOVERNMENT'S LIKE, AS LONG AS THEY HAVE WATER AND NO SAND!...
41B

DON'T GO! WAIT!!!

SOON, BOOMVILLE WAS NOTHING MORE THAN A MEMORY...
IT WAS TAKEN DOWN AS QUICKLY AS IT HAD BEEN PUT UP...

HEY! THEY TOOK THE WALL WHERE I HUNG MY CLOTHES!
HOTEL

HERE! WE'RE CLOSING THE BANK! I'LL HAND BACK THE DEPOSITORS' MONEY! HURRY UP—I WANT TO GO!...
BANK

FOR SALE FOR $1,000 $100 $10
THIS LAND SOLD FOR $5,000 LAST WEEK

IT'S ALL OVER!
LOOK! THE UNDERTAKER'S GIVING UP ON US! HE'S LEAVING TOO!!...

MAIN STREET
IT'S A BIT SAD, EH, OLD DOPEY?...

THE SANDSTORM BLEW ITSELF OUT... A FEW ABANDONED RUINS SHOWED THAT BOOMVILLE HAD EXISTED, THAT A NOISY LIFE AND GREAT ADVENTURES HAD LIVENED UP THIS NOW-DESERTED PLACE... THE "BOOM" TOWN WAS NOTHING MORE THAN A "GHOST" TOWN...

THE RESPONSE CAME BACK QUICKLY...

WESTERN UNION
WASHINGTON DC
LUCKY LUKE (OKLAHOMA STATE LINE)
REPRESENTATIVE OF THE GOVERNMENT
EN ROUTE FOR OKLAHOMA STOP
ORGANISE A MEETING WITH TRIBAL
CHIEFS WHO SOLD TERRITORY

IT SHOULD BE NOTED THAT LARGE OIL RESERVES WERE DISCOVERED SOON AFTER IN OKLAHOMA'S INCREDIBLY RICH GROUND... THE NATIVE AMERICANS QUIETLY BECAME MULTI-BILLIONAIRES...

COMING SOON

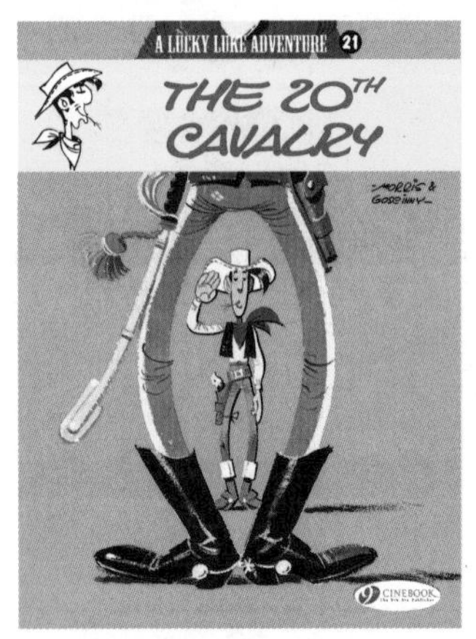

FEBRUARY 2010

APRIL 2010

JUNE 2010

AUGUST 2010